Copyright © 1987 by bohem press—Zurich, Recklinghausen, Vienna, Paris.
Original title: "Der Grosste Schatz"
Distributed in Canada by Vanwell Publishing, St. Catharines, Ont.
Published and distributed in USA by Picture Book Studio, Saxonville, MA.
All rights reserved.
Printed in Hong Kong.

Library of Congress Cataloging in Publication Data
Lobato, Arcadio.
The greatest treasure.
Originally published in Spanish.
Summary: It is time for the witches to choose a new queen and it
will be the witch who finds the most special treasure.
[1. Witches—Fiction] I. Title
PZ7.L7788Gr 1989 [E] 89-3612
ISBN 0-88708-093-6

The Greatest Treasure

Arcadio Lobato

Picture Book Studio

In the Land of Witches, old Queen Druscilla had ruled for 400 years, and now it was time for her to choose the next queen. She decided that this time it would be different. There would be a contest—a great treasure hunt.

Meera wasn't really interested. She was happy just to stay at home, reading her books and studying the stars.

But her friend Ernest the raven wouldn't hear of it. "Let's go! You would be a great queen, and the treasure hunt will be fun."

Meera didn't really think so,
but she set off on her
broom anyway, with
Ernest flying
close behind.

As they flew along, Ernest recited the queen's proclamation for the tenth time:

"Treasures great and treasures small,
You must find the best of all:
Something precious, something rare,
Something found by one who cares.

If you wish to rule the witches,
Which is rather fun to do,
You must know which treasure this is.
Finding it is up to you."

Suddenly, with no warning—"CCRAACKK!"—Meera's broom broke, and she plunked down onto a little island.

"Drat!" squawked Ernest. "Now we'll never find a treasure, and you won't be the queen."

Meera said, "Oh Ernest, calm down, calm down. Look, all it needs is a twist and a pull and a tidy little knot…there. All fixed. I'm just glad that the island was here!"

But the island was not an island. It was a sleeping whale.

First he felt their footsteps on his back, and it kind of tickled him in his sleep. Then he heard their voices, and he woke up suddenly and plunged forward.

Meera guessed at once. "A whale! How wonderful! Let's follow him."

"But how?" asked the raven. "He'll be much too fast, and besides we need to stay above water so we can breathe."

So the witch quickly said,

"Zee, za, zo,
  Down we go in the deep blue sea.
  High or low—
  Let air be there for the bird and me."

As these magic words were spoken, they dove below the waves. In the depths of the sea—far, far below the light of day—swam fish that glistened like golden stars.

The raven squawked and pointed: "Look! There's our treasure! No one has ever seen such fish!"

Meera didn't even seem to hear him. She waved her arms and called out, "Mr. Whale, here we are! Please, wait for us...come now, don't run away." But the whale swam off.

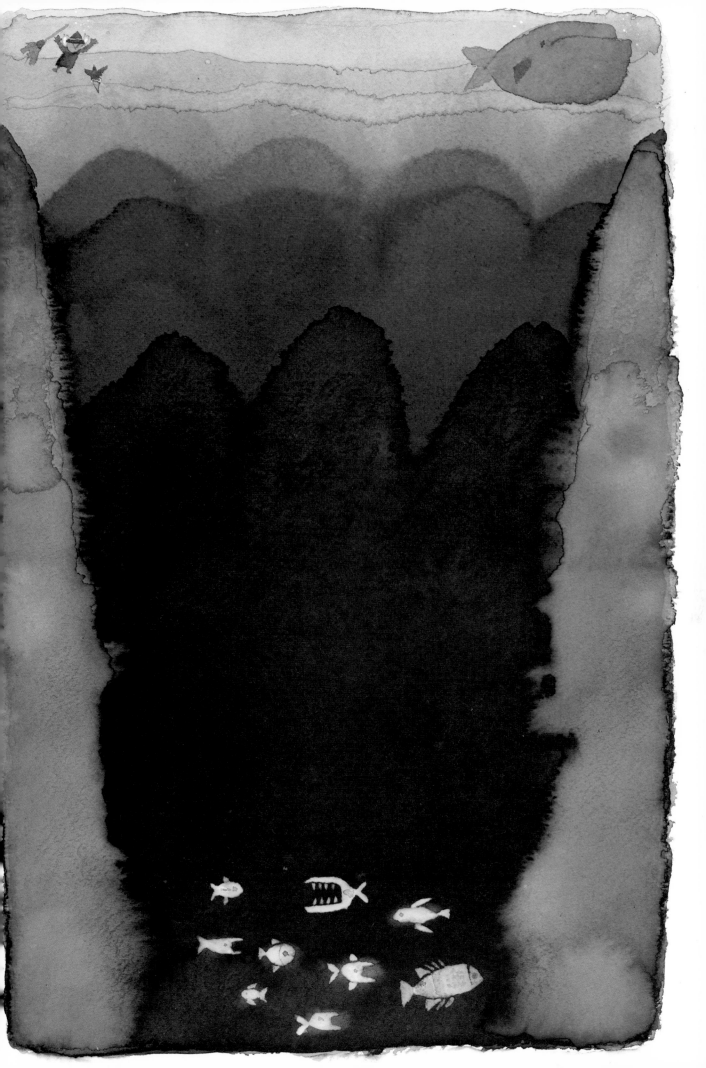

"Meera, stop!" said Ernest. "Why chase an old whale? We should be looking for treasure. Besides, you haven't even seen the fluorescent fishes. And look there, a sunken ship! It could be a pirate ship loaded down with gold and jewels."

But Meera paid no attention and swam ahead.

As they followed along trying to catch up with the whale, they
came upon an ancient sunken city. Houses and streets, temples
and palaces were just lying there waiting to be explored.

"Think of all the treasures we could find there!" said Ernest.

"But to find them we would have to stop," said Meera, "and the whale is not stopping. We must swim as the whale swims, and he swims very quickly. Hurry up!"

Speeding through the water, Ernest called out, "Meera, look! Look at the bright coral, and the oysters with all those glowing pearls. Why, it's a king's ransom, and all we have to do is swoop down and pick it up. It's wonderful! Please, Meera, must we go on with this swimming and swimming and swimming?"

"Now which way did that fellow go?" said Meera. "I've lost sight of him. Ernest, if you would swim more and talk less, we just might catch up to our whale. Now let's go!"

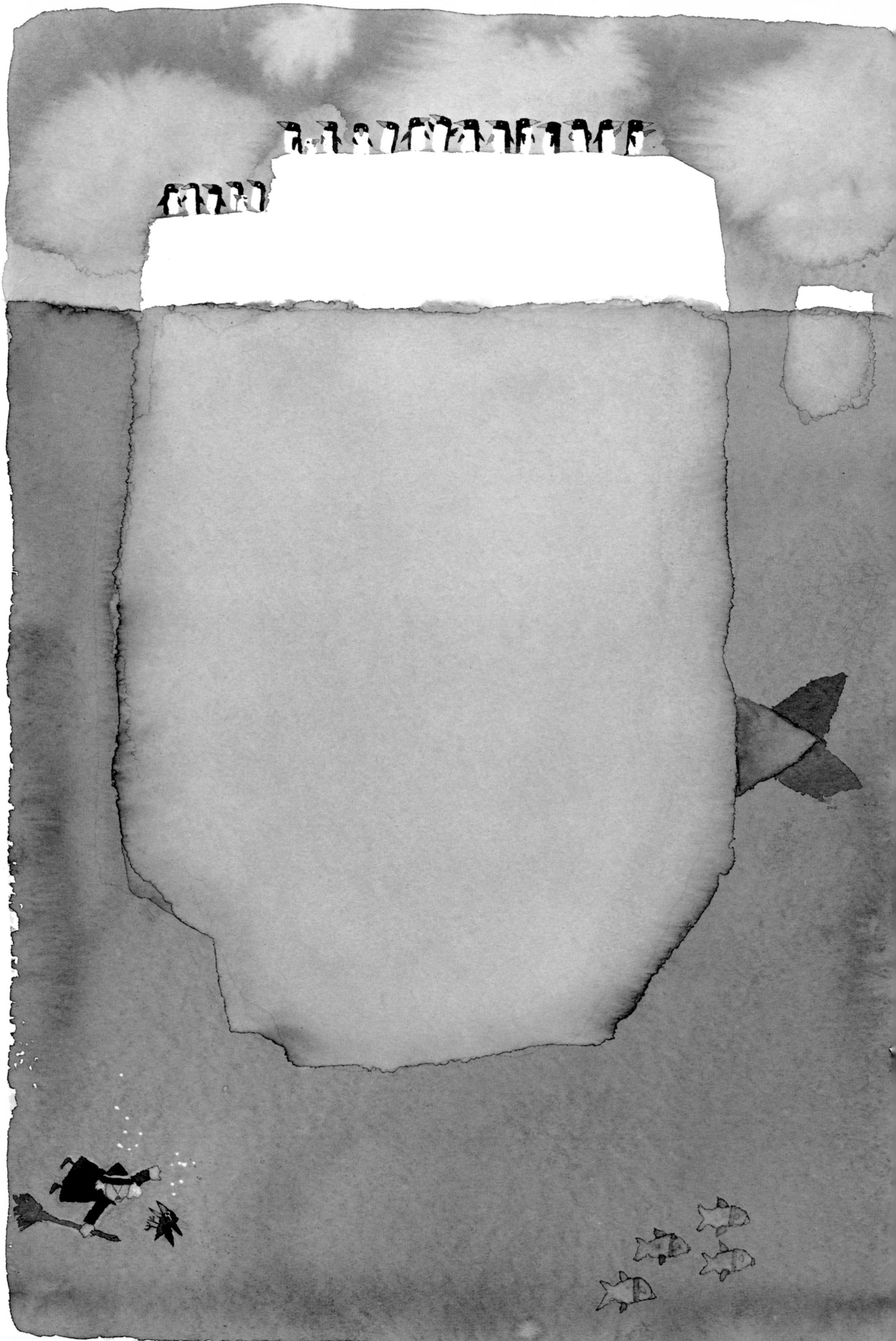

Meera and Ernest searched on and on until they reached the cold seas near the South pole.

The raven finally stopped. "Enough!" he shouted. "Meera, why are you chasing this whale? Are you trying to trap him like a hunter?"

"Ernest! I would never hurt a whale," said Meera. "All I want to do is talk with him for a while. I'm only chasing him because I want to be friends with him and invite him to come back to visit our city. Now Ernest, wouldn't you like to be the only raven in the whole world that has talked with a real whale?"

The raven thought for a minute and then said, "Yes, I guess it would be fun to know a whale…but if we can't find him, can we go back and get some of those pearls anyway?"

Suddenly, before Meera could answer, the whale was there beside them. It had been hiding behind the iceberg, and he had heard everything they said.

"When you came after me," said the whale, "I was scared. But now that I know why you were chasing me, I would be very happy to be your friend. I would even like to visit your city, but it is a long, long way back, and I am quite tired from all the swimming."

"Leave that to me," cried the happy witch. "We'll all *fly* home.
Ernest can fly because he is a raven, I can fly because I am
a witch, and for you, my large friend, I have a magic spell:

As penguins fly in the watery deep,
And moonlight floats on the sea,

Spread flippers and fins
In the clouds and the winds,
And swim through the sky with me!"

The whale swept up through the waves and into the sky,
light as a seagull feather.

They flew together over icebergs and oceans until they finally arrived back at the Land of Witches. All the other witches were amazed to see the huge whale flying along with Ernest and Meera.

The ceremony to choose the new queen was just beginning. The witches had brought all their treasures, and the old queen looked thoughtfully at the glittering pile in front of her.

Then she spoke. "Witches, listen. All these treasures here are quite beautiful, but they can all be bought with gold: the jewels, the rare fabrics, the precious carvings…everything!

"Only Meera and Ernest have returned with something truly wonderful: a friend. And that is a treasure which no one can buy."

She placed the golden crown on Meera's head. "Here is our new queen. Let the celebration begin!"

During the magic of the evening, the witches sang and danced and feasted in the gleam of the firelight.

And for the rest of the night, the whale told them the ancient tales of the sea.